A *Little, Brown* Book

First published in Great Britain in 1992
by Little, Brown and Company

A CIP catalogue record for this book is available from
the British Library.

ISBN 0 316 90393 0

Printed and bound in Italy by Graphicom SRL.

Little, Brown and Company (UK) Limited
165 Great Dover Street
London SE1 4YA

Clangers

The Iron Chicken

STORY BY OLIVER POSTGATE
PICTURES BY PETER FIRMIN

LITTLE, BROWN AND COMPANY

"WAKE UP! Wake up, Tiny Clanger!" whistled Small
Clanger. "Wake up! Major Clanger is going to let off a new
rocket!"

Tiny Clanger was asleep in her little round nest in the
wall of the big cave but Small Clanger's loud whistling
woke her up. She lifted her ears off her eyes – which, as
you know, is how Clangers open their eyes – and lifted up
the flap which was the door of her nest.

Then, still curled up in a ball – which, as you also know, is how Clangers always sleep – she tipped herself out of the nest and rolled down the slope to where Small Clanger was waiting.

There she uncurled and stood up.

"You are the laziest Tiny Clanger in the whole galaxy!" whistled her brother, Small Clanger.

"I am the ONLY Tiny Clanger in the galaxy!" she replied proudly.

"Pull! . . . Pull! . . . Pull! . . . Pull! . . ." Tiny and Small could hear the other Clangers hooting and whistling as they pulled something through the big door and out into the open.

They ran to help.

The thing they were pulling was one of Major Clanger's inventions.

Major Clanger was Small and Tiny Clanger's father. He was also the biggest and the strongest and the cleverest of all the Clangers who lived on, in and under the small blue moon which was their home.

That day Major Clanger had invented and made two rockets. He liked to invent rockets. These were not rockets for space travel or for sending messages. These rockets were just for fun.

The Clangers set one of the new rockets in the rocket-launcher. Major Clanger connected the ignition cable and began the count-down.

"Ten . . . nine . . . eight . . . seven . . ."

Major Clanger's ears began to droop because he was feeling nervous – perhaps it would not work!

"Three . . . two . . . one . . ."

WHOOOOOOOOOOSH!

"We have lift-off!" he hooted.

The Clangers all looked up into the black sky.

They saw the rocket burst and throw out clouds and clouds of stars, fountains of fizzy sparkles and many-coloured trees of light which slowly grew and spread and glided across the sky.

They clapped and whistled with joy.

"More! . . . More! . . . More! Please may we let off the other one, please!" they hooted.

So Major Clanger let them set up the other rocket. He counted it down and . . . *WHOOOOOSH!* . . . up it went.

But this rocket did not burst into stars, this rocket went . . . *ker-CLANG!* It had hit something in the sky.

WHEEEEP-clonk, CLONK. Things were falling all around them.

"EVERYBODY BELOW!" shouted Major Clanger and, without waiting to argue, the Clangers dived for their holes and pulled down the metal lids.

Clink-clank, clink-clonk, clink, clinkle-clankle-clonk!

The Clangers lifted the lids and looked out.

Lots of long silvery strips and plates and panels of metal had fallen from the sky.

It was obviously a thing of some sort but it was all in pieces. So they carried it down into the big cave and tried to put it together again.

The Clangers could see that the thing was quite easy to put together but when it was put together it was not easy to see what it was supposed to be. They stepped back to look at it.

The thing scraped and clanked and creaked as it lifted itself on two iron feet and spread its iron wings.

"Eeeeeur," it grunted in a scratchy voice. "Thankyou-very-much, thankyou-very-much!"

It was an iron chicken.

"How-do-you-do? How-do-you-do?" she clucked as she bowed and turned and bowed again. She was certainly a very polite and well-mannered bird.

"How do you do? How do you do?" whistled the Clangers politely as they bowed to the Iron Chicken.

"Thankyou-very-much," clucked the Iron Chicken and she turned and walked away into the caves.

The Clangers heard her iron joints clinking and clanking as she walked away, and they were amazed.

"Well I never! How unusual! Goodness gracious!" they whistled and hooted to each other.

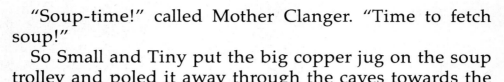

"Soup-time!" called Mother Clanger. "Time to fetch soup!"

So Small and Tiny put the big copper jug on the soup trolley and poled it away through the caves towards the soup wells.

"Look!" shouted Tiny. "Look! Look at that!"

The Iron Chicken was standing by the soup wells eating the copper leaves from the copper-leaf trees.

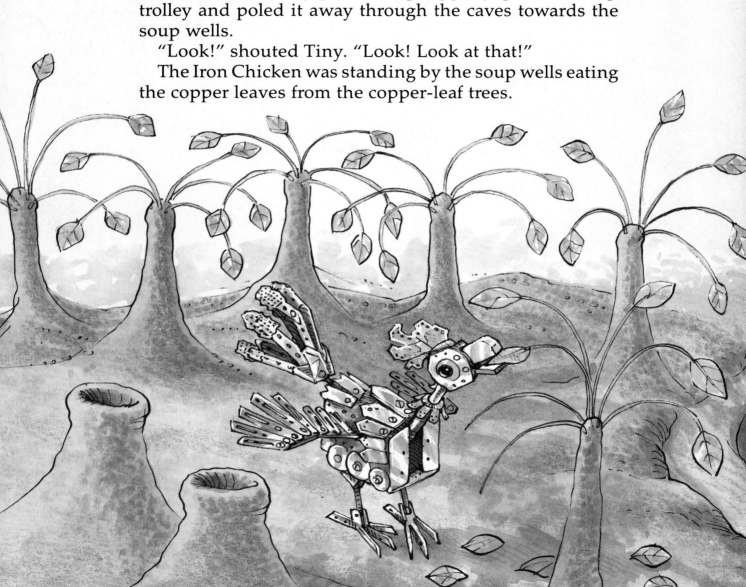

"She should not be doing that!" said Small Clanger. "Those leaves are not for eating!"

"She shoulddle not be doodling that!" said the Soup Dragon in her burbly voice. "That's nottle polite!"

No, the Iron Chicken was not being polite. It is not polite to eat the leaves off the Clangers' copper-leaf trees. But then the Iron Chicken did something that was much more impolite.

She stretched out her long neck made of iron piping and put her head right down into the soup well. Then she started to suck up the soup like a vacuum-cleaner.

The Soup Dragon was furious. She hit the chicken with her big wooden spoon.

THUMP . . . "COME OUT!" she shouted.

THUMP . . . "COME OUT!"

THUMP . . . "COME OUT!"

The Iron Chicken did not seem to feel the blows but perhaps that was because she was made of iron. When she had drunk all the soup she wanted she stood up straight and looked at them.

"Thankyou-very-much, thankyou-very-much, thankyou-very-much!" she clucked.

The Iron Chicken walked past the copper-leaf trees and straight on, straight into the wall of the cave. The soft rock which the Clangers' moon is made of crumbled away as she pecked and pushed her way through it, leaving a big black hole and a pile of broken rubble.

"That was a very rude thing to do," said Small Clanger. "Walking through other people's walls is not a polite thing to do."

Small and Tiny collected their jug of green soup and poled the soup trolley away.

Mother Clanger had cooked some delicious blue-string pudding, which is the Clangers' favourite food. As you know, it is their only food, apart from green soup, so they are lucky it is also their favourite food.

The pudding-pan was in the middle of the dinner-block and all the Clangers were there, ready to start eating, when Tiny Clanger looked up at the roof of the big cave.

"Look out!" she whistled. "It is falling in!"

The Clangers looked up and then they ran! The rocky ceiling of their cave was breaking up.

Large chunks of the rock fell down and among them fell the Iron Chicken. She was quite safe and feeling hungry.

"Ooooooh!" she clucked, "Blue-string pudding, my favourite pudding!"

The Iron Chicken climbed right on to the dinner-block. She reached out her neck and helped herself to beakfuls of the Clangers' dinner.

Major Clanger was very, very angry.

"You can't do that!" he shouted. "That is our dinner you are eating!"

"Erw?" asked the Iron Chicken.

"That is our ceiling you just fell out of!" shouted Major Clanger.

"Er . . . was it?" clucked the Iron Chicken.

"You are a rude, nasty, ill-mannered iron bird!" hooted Major Clanger.

"Oh dear," sighed the Iron Chicken.

"You are not polite! You are rude! We do not want you to be here!" shouted Major Clanger.

The Iron Chicken pulled her iron neck into her iron body and crouched down. Tiny Clanger thought she had never seen anybody look so sad and sorry.

"Do not talk to her like that!" said Tiny Clanger to her father, "She does not know that what she has done is not polite."

Tiny Clanger took a little wreath of golden leaves and put it around the neck of the Iron Chicken.

"You are welcome Iron Chicken," she said. "I am pleased that you are here."

The Iron Chicken looked happier.

Then Tiny Clanger climbed up and sat beside the Chicken. She explained to her that, on a small moon, Clangers, and chickens, needed to behave politely. They should not knock down the walls or drop in through the ceiling, and should not eat other people's dinner or drink soup straight from the Soup Dragon's well. If they behaved politely they would be most welcome and Clangers would be their friends.

The Iron Chicken was pleased to hear this.

"Will you be my friend?" she asked.

"Yes! I would love to be your friend!" whistled Tiny Clanger happily.

"OOOoooh!" The Chicken was so pleased to hear this that she stood up and flapped her wings.

She turned around three times, clucked loudly and then – CLANG! – she laid one large iron egg.

"That is for you," she said to Tiny Clanger, "because you are my friend!"

Tiny Clanger was delighted. "Ooooh!" she hooted, "What a lovely present!" though to tell the truth she wasn't at all sure what she would do with a large iron egg.

The Iron Chicken said it had been a great pleasure meeting them all but it was time for her to fly back to her untidy nest somewhere out in space.

She said goodbye most politely to the Clangers and, as she ran across the curved outside of the moon, flapped her wings and took off into the dark sky, they stood and waved goodbye to her.

"Goodbye Iron Chicken! Come and see us again soon!" they whistled.

"You see," said Tiny Clanger to her father, "she was a nice chicken really. You just have to be a bit friendly, that's all."